WALT DISNEY'S
THREE LITTLE PIGS

Retold by
JANET CAMPBELL

Illustrated by
GIL DiCICCO

DISNEY PRESS
NEW YORK

Library of Congress Catalog Card Number: 92-53443
ISBN 1-56282-381-7/1-56282-382-5 (lib. bdg.)

Walt Disney's
THREE LITTLE PIGS

Once upon a time, there were three little pigs who were ready to leave home and seek their fortunes in the wide, wide world.

5

The first little pig, whose
name was Fifer, wrapped
his flute and his lunch in a
blue bandanna. He tied it
to a stick and threw it over
his shoulder.

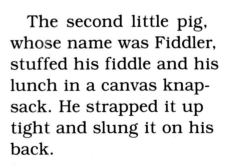

The second little pig,
whose name was Fiddler,
stuffed his fiddle and his
lunch in a canvas knap-
sack. He strapped it up
tight and slung it on his
back.

The third little pig, whose name was Practical, got an old suit-case down from the attic. He packed seven pairs of socks, seven changes of underwear, two pairs of pajamas, a toothbrush, tooth-paste, and soap. He tucked his lunch into one corner, leaving just enough room for his piggy bank.

"Now listen carefully," said Practical Pig to his two brothers. "The very first thing we must do in the wide, wide world is build ourselves stout little houses to keep out the big bad wolf."

"Oh, Practical," said Fifer Pig. "All you ever think about is work. We want to have fun in the wide, wide world."

"That's right," said Fiddler Pig. "Besides, we're not afraid of any big bad wolf."

Fifer and Fiddler began to dance around the kitchen table on the tips of their pointy pig toes, singing:

Who's afraid of the big bad wolf,
  big bad wolf,
  big bad wolf.
Who's afraid of the big bad wolf,
  Tra-la-la-la-laaaa!

Out the door and down the road went those two little pigs,
dancing and prancing and singing at the top of their squeaky
pig voices. Practical Pig ran panting along behind, his heavy
suitcase banging about his ankles.

They hadn't gone far when Fifer Pig saw a great bundle of straw in the middle of a field.

"Just what I need to build a little house!" he exclaimed. "And it'll be as easy as *A, B, C*!" So he set to work immediately to build himself a house of straw.

"Good-bye and good luck!" called his brothers, and off they went down the road into the wide, wide world.

They hadn't gone far when Fiddler Pig saw a big pile of sticks beside the road. "Just what I need to build *my* little house!" he exclaimed. "And it'll be as simple as one, two, three!" So he went right to work to build himself a house of sticks.

"Good-bye and good luck!" called Practical Pig, and off he went down the road into the wide, wide world.

Practical Pig hadn't gone far when he found a perfect place for his little house, up on a hill with a view all around, the better to see the big bad wolf coming.

He counted out just enough change to buy a good supply of bricks and set right to work to build himself a stout little wolf-proof house.

By this time, Fifer Pig had already finished his house of straw. It was a round, cozy little house with a straw chair and a straw mat at the door. Fifer Pig was so pleased with himself for doing such a good job, he sat down under a tree to admire his work. He got out his lunch and ate up every bite.

Then he took out his flute and began to dance and sing:

I built my house of straw,
I built my house of hay,
I toot my flute,
I don't give a hoot,
And I play around all day.

14

Fiddler Pig had now finished his house of sticks, too. It was a square, snug little house with a bench of sticks outside and a horseshoe over the door for good luck. Fiddler Pig was so proud of himself for doing such a splendid job, he sat down on a big rock to admire his work. He got out his lunch and ate up every bite.

Then he took out his fiddle and began to dance and sing:

I built my house of sticks,
I built my house of twigs,
With a hey diddle diddle
I play on the fiddle
While I dance all kinds of jigs.

Now Practical Pig was still hard at work building his house of bricks. And as he worked he sang:

I build my house of stones,
I build my house of bricks,
I've had no chance to sing and dance,
For work and play don't mix.

Along came his brothers, dancing and singing at the top of their squeaky pig voices. When they saw Practical Pig, they laughed until their sides ached.

"Work, work, work," giggled Fifer Pig. "I'm glad I built my house of straw. It was so much easier."

"Work, work, work," giggled Fiddler Pig. "I'm glad I built my house of sticks. It was so much faster."

Practical Pig wiped his forehead with a bandanna. "Easier and faster are not always better," he said. "You'll be sorry when the big bad wolf comes to your door!" He stuffed his bandanna back in his pocket and started to build his chimney.

"The big bad wolf?" laughed his brothers. "We're not afraid of any big bad wolf!" And they struck up their song and danced off down the road:

Who's afraid of the big bad wolf,
  big bad wolf,
  big bad wolf.
Who's afraid of the big bad wolf,
  Tra-la-la-la-laaaa!

Fifer and Fiddler danced all the way down the road and into the shady woods. There they stopped, giggling and gasping for breath. They had never had so much fun as being out and about in the wide, wide world.

Suddenly there was a rustling of bushes. The two little pigs held their breath and listened.

Then there was a crackling of twigs. The two little pigs turned their heads and stared.

Right before their eyes, the biggest, baddest wolf those two little pigs could have ever imagined leapt out from behind a tree!

The two little pigs jumped in the air, squealing with fright. Then home they went as fast as their stumpy pig legs could carry them, with the big bad wolf snapping at their heels.

Fifer Pig ran straight to his little straw house, pulled in his welcome mat, slammed the door, and pushed a table, a stool, and a chair up against it to hold it tight.

BANG, BANG, BANG! The big bad wolf knocked on the door of the little straw house with his big furry paw until the house shook.

"Open the door and let me in," growled the wicked wolf.

"Not by the hair of my chinny-chin-chin," cried Fifer Pig.

"Then I'll huff, and I'll puff, and I'll *blow* your house in," snarled the big bad wolf.

And he huffed, and he puffed...and he blew that little straw house right in. Away flew the walls! Down came the roof!

Fifer Pig scrambled out from under the pile of straw that had been his roof and ran, squealing, all the way to Fiddler Pig's house, with the big bad wolf right on his heels.

Fiddler Pig came out of his house just in time to pull his brother into the house. He slammed the door right in the face of the big bad wolf.

RATTLE, RATTLE, RATTLE! The wolf shook and shook the door. The two little pigs hid under the rug, quaking with fear.

Suddenly everything was very quiet, because that wicked wolf was thinking of a way to trick those two little pigs.

"Well," said the big bad wolf finally, loud enough for the two little pigs to hear, "they're too smart for me. I guess I'll go home."

Galump, galump, galump. The big bad wolf slapped his knees to make the sound of footsteps. Then he hid behind a hedge of sunflowers and waited.

Fifer Pig and Fiddler Pig crawled out from under the rug and listened anxiously at the keyhole. "He's gone!" they said. Then they giggled and shook hands and began to sing:

Who's afraid of the big bad wolf,
  big bad wolf,
  big bad wolf...

BANG, BANG, BANG! There was a knocking at the door.

The two little pigs jumped with fright. "Who's there?" they squealed, peering through the cracks in the stick walls. There at the door, lying in a wicker basket, was the scraggliest, silliest looking creature they had ever seen.

"I'm a poor little sheep with no place to sleep," whined the creature, who was really the big bad wolf in disguise. "Please open the door and let me in."

"Not by the hair of our chinny-chin-chin," said Fifer Pig and Fiddler Pig. "You can't fool us with that old sheepskin."

"Then I'll huff, and I'll puff, and I'll *blow* your house in!" snarled the big bad wolf, jumping out of the basket and throwing off the sheepskin.

And he huffed and he puffed…and he huffed and he puffed…and he blew that little stick house right in! All that was left standing was the front door, because Fifer Pig and Fiddler Pig were braced against it.

Slowly they opened their eyes. They looked up. The roof was gone! They looked around. The walls were gone! They opened the door. The wolf came pouncing through!

And away ran the two little pigs, as fast as they could, with the big bad wolf snatching at their curly pig tails.

Practical Pig had finally finished his sturdy little house of bricks. He was sitting on his porch waiting for the soup kettle to boil.

Suddenly Fifer Pig and Fiddler Pig came dashing up the hill, rushed past their brother, ran into his house, and dove under the bed.

Practical Pig had just enough time to run into the house behind them and chain the door tight.

He looked at his two foolish brothers quivering under the bed and shook his head. "You can come out now," he said. "We are safe and sound in my sturdy little brick house."

Then he sat down at his brick piano and began to play and sing:

Who's afraid of the big bad wolf,
  big bad wolf,
  big bad wolf...

BANG, BANG, BANG! There was a loud knocking at the door. Fifer and Fiddler Pig dove back under the bed.

But not Practical Pig. "Who's there?" he asked calmly.

"It's the brush salesman," said a voice outside the door. "I have a free sample for you."

Practical Pig opened the door just as far as the chain would allow. "Thank you," he said, grabbing the brush from the paw of the salesman, who was really the big bad wolf in disguise.

Quickly the wolf stuck his large furry foot through the opening. *SMACK!* Practical Pig hit the wolf's foot with the brush. The wolf yelped. *CRACK!* Practical Pig hit the wolf's head with the brush. The wolf howled. Then Practical Pig slammed the door shut and laughed.

"All right," snarled the big bad wolf. "By the hair of *my* chinny-chin-chin, I'll huff, and I'll puff, and I'll *blow* your house in!"

So he huffed and he puffed,

and he huffed and he puffed,

and he huffed and he puffed some more....

Then he stopped to catch his breath.

And then he huffed and he puffed until his face turned blue, but he could not blow that sturdy little brick house in!

So he sat down to think.

Suddenly it was very quiet outside. Fifer Pig and Fiddler Pig came out from under the bed, dusted themselves off, and began to laugh. Then Fifer took up his flute, Fiddler took up his fiddle, and they began to dance and sing:

Who's afraid of the
big bad wolf,
big bad wolf,
big bad wolf.
Who's afraid of the...

"Hush!" said Practical Pig. "I hear something."
The two little pigs stopped playing. Sure enough, there was just the hint of a scrambling up the brick wall, then just the whisper of a sliding across the roof.

"The chimney!" squeaked Practical Pig. He ran to the fireplace and snatched the lid from the soup kettle.

Suddenly there was a frantic scratching on the chimney walls, and with a loud *SPLASHHH! HISSSS!* the big bad wolf fell right into the pot of boiling water.

"*OUCH!*" he cried. "*OOOCH!*" he screamed. "*YEEEOOW!*" he howled. And then that big bad wolf shot straight back up the chimney and went yelping, "*AH-WOOO! AH-WOOO! AH-WOOO!*" down the road all the way back to the woods, where he belonged.

The very next day, Practical Pig, Fifer Pig, and Fiddler Pig got to work and built two more sturdy little brick houses. And that big bad wolf never came near those three little pigs again.